I Am

Why Two Little Words Mean So Much

DR. WAYNE W. DYER

with Kristina Tracy

HAY HOUSE, INC.
Carlsbad, California • New York City
London • Sydney • Johannesburg
Vancouver • Hong Kong • New Delhi

Illustrated by
Stacy Heller Budnick

Published and distributed in the United States by: Hay House, Inc.: www.hayhouse.com • *Published and distributed in Australia by:* Hay House Australia Pty. Ltd.: www.hayhouse.com.au • *Published and distributed in the United Kingdom by:* Hay House UK, Ltd.: www.hayhouse.co.uk • *Published and distributed in the Republic of South Africa by:* Hay House SA (Pty), Ltd.: www.hayhouse.co.za • *Distributed in Canada by:* Raincoast: www.raincoast.com • *Published in India by:* Hay House Publishers India: www.hayhouse.co.in

Cover design, interior design, and editorial assistance: Jenny Richards • *Illustrations:* © Stacy Heller Budnick

Library of Congress Control Number: 2011944404

ISBN: 978-1-4019-3975-5
Digital ISBN: 978-1-4019-3976-2

15 14 13 12   4 3 2 1
1st edition, March 2012

Printed in China

Dear Parents and Teachers,

I am so excited to share this new book with you and your children. My studies and teachings over the past several years have led me to write a book for adults called *Wishes Fulfilled*. I have taken the most important concept from *Wishes Fulfilled* and created this children's book. The concept is that God is not separate from us but is actually an energy living inside of us. Once we become aware of this energy, we can help it to grow and expand and bring happiness to ourselves and others. What I hope to offer children with this book is the understanding that they are a part of God and God is a part of them. I like to explain it like this: Imagine God as the ocean. If you take a bucket of water out of the ocean, is it still the ocean? Yes! God is the ocean, and we are the buckets of water drawn from the ocean—separate, but one.

I named this book *I Am* because of the incredibly powerful meaning of those two words. How we finish the sentence that begins with "I am" makes all the difference in the life we create for ourselves and how close or far away we are from the part of us that is God. I have included more on the use of "I am" at the end of the book. My wish is that each one of us comes to recognize and connect to the amazing gift that is God's love.

Dr. Wayne W. Dyer

Hello, my friend—
    do you know who I am?

Listen carefully to this
    rhyme, and try to
        guess if you can!

Do I live in the clouds
so far away?

Or is a temple or a church
the place that I stay?

I am in those places,
        yes, that is true,
But only because I am in you.

We are not separate—
wherever you are, I am there.

I am in your mind and your heart . . .
I am everywhere!

You're like a candle lit
　　from my bright flame.

My light is your light—
　　we are one and the same.

I am everything that is good
and everything that is real,

I am the source of
all the warmth you feel.

I am the part of you that
shares and gives from
your heart.

I am **the inspiration**
behind your music,
sports, and art.

I am the voice that you hear
when you are quiet and still,
I am the little bird
on your windowsill.

I am in everyone you see—
young or old, big or small,

Believe it or not,
I am in them all.

Who can I be? I AM GOD, your best friend.

And there's really no line

where you start and I end.

Did you hear what I said—**are you listening?**
For you will be amazed at what this
knowledge will bring.

You will live your life knowing it is never just you,
and that **we are together**
in all that you do.

Along the way,
you will find
great happiness
and love,

And you'll learn that
wishes come true
from within,
not above.

So, don't look to the sky
      when you're looking for me,
Look right at **yourself** . . .
            and that's where I'll be!

The Meaning of "I Am"

As you read this book, you may have noticed that many of the sentences start with the words *I am*. These are two of the most powerful words you can use to begin a sentence. The important thing is what words you use to finish that sentence. Anytime you start a sentence with *I am*, you are creating what you are and what you want to be. At the same time, you are also showing whether or not you are connected to the energy of God inside of you. So, if you sometimes say, "I am bad at this, I am ugly, I am stupid," these words take you farther and farther away from the part of you that is God. When you choose to say, "I am happy, I am kind, I am perfect," you help the light of God inside you to grow and shine. Try saying some *I am* sentences. See how different words make you feel.

I am_____

I am_____

I am_____

I am_____

I am_____

We hope you enjoyed this Hay House book.
If you'd like to receive our online catalog featuring additional information
on Hay House books and products, or if you'd like to find out more
about the Hay Foundation, please contact:

Hay House, Inc.
P.O. Box 5100
Carlsbad, CA 92018-5100

(760) 431-7695 or (800) 654-5126
(760) 431-6948 (fax) or (800) 650-5115 (fax)
www.hayhouse.com® • **www.hayfoundation.org**

Published and distributed in Australia by: Hay House Australia Pty. Ltd., 18/36 Ralph St., Alexandria NSW 2015
Phone: 612-9669-4299 • Fax: 612-9669-4144 • www.hayhouse.com.a

Published and distributed in the United Kingdom by: Hay House UK, Ltd., 292B Kensal Rd., London W10 5BE
Phone: 44-20-8962-1230 • Fax: 44-20-8962-1239 • www.hayhouse.co.uk

Published and distributed in the Republic of South Africa by: Hay House SA (Pty), Ltd., P.O. Box 990, Witkoppen 2068
Phone/Fax: 27-11-467-8904 • info@hayhouse.co.za • www.hayhouse.co.za

Published in India by: Hay House Publishers India, Muskaan Complex, Plot No. 3, B-2, Vasant Kunj, New Delhi 110 070
Phone: 91-11-4176-1620 • Fax: 91-11-4176-1630 • www.hayhouse.co.in

Distributed in Canada by: Raincoast, 9050 Shaughnessy St., Vancouver, B.C. V6P 6E5 •
Phone: (604) 323-7100 • Fax: (604) 323-2600 • www.raincoast.com

Take Your Soul on a Vacation

Visit **www.HealYourLife.com**® to regroup, recharge, and reconnect with your own magnificence.
Featuring blogs, mind-body-spirit news, and life-changing wisdom from Louise Hay and friends.